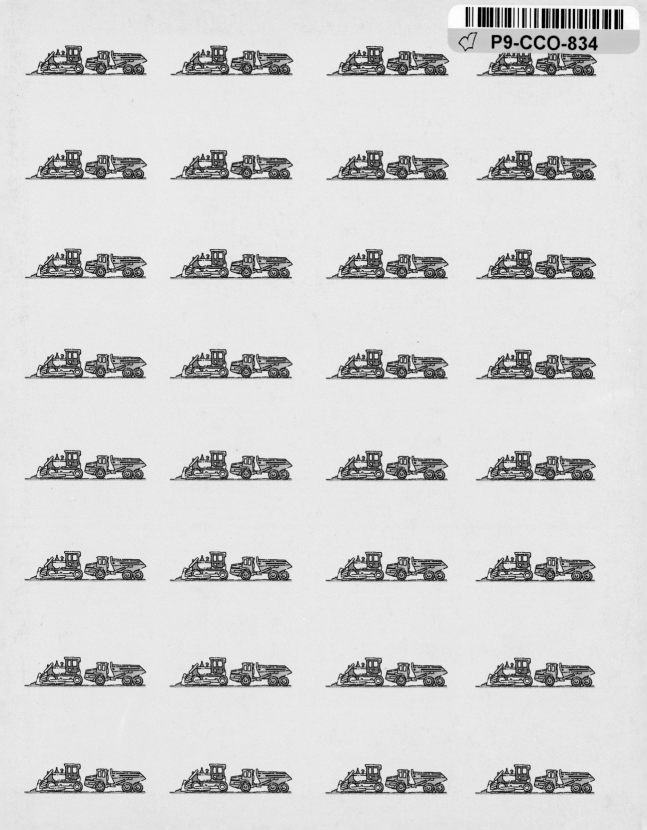

A DORLING KINDERSLEY BOOK

Written by Angela Royston
Photography by Tim Ridley
Illustrations by Jane Cradock-Watson and Dave Hopkins
Models by Conrad GMBH
Model consultant Ted Taylor

LITTLE SIMON MERCHANDISE
An imprint of Simon & Schuster Children's Publishing Division
1230 Avenue of the Americas
New York, New York 10020
Copyright © 1991 by Dorling Kindersley Limited, London
All rights reserved including the right of reproduction
in whole or in part in any form.
LITTLE SIMON and colophon are trademarks of Simon & Schuster.

Eye Openers™
First published in Great Britain in 1991
by Dorling Kindersley Limited,
9 Henrietta Street, London WC2E 8PS

Reproduced by Colourscan, Singapore
Printed and bound in Italy by L.E.G.O., Vicenza

8 9 10

ISBN 0-689-71516-1

Library of Congress CIP data is available.

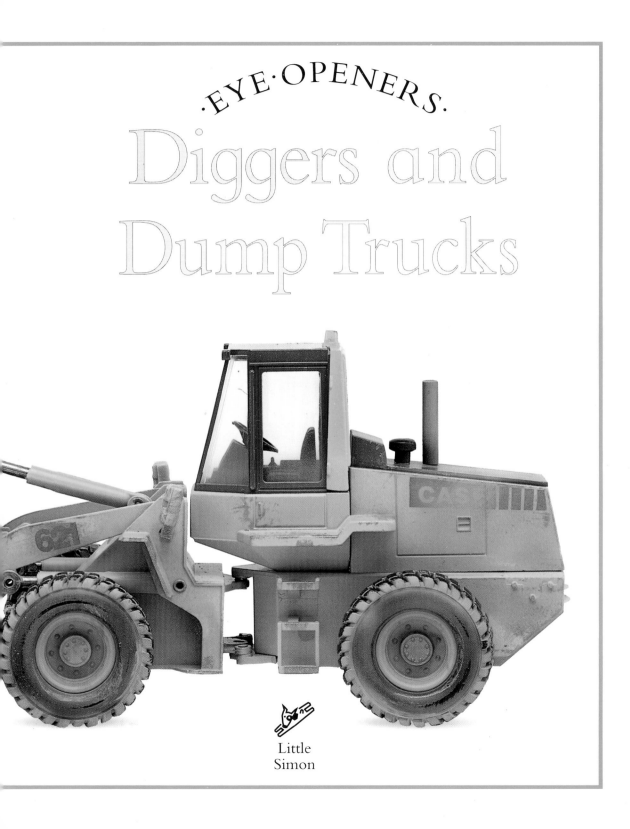

·EYE·OPENERS·

Diggers and Dump Trucks

Little
Simon

Bulldozer

A bulldozer flattens the ground at a building site. Its huge blade pushes away stones and dirt. The crawler tracks spread its weight so it doesn't sink into the mud.

exhaust
stack

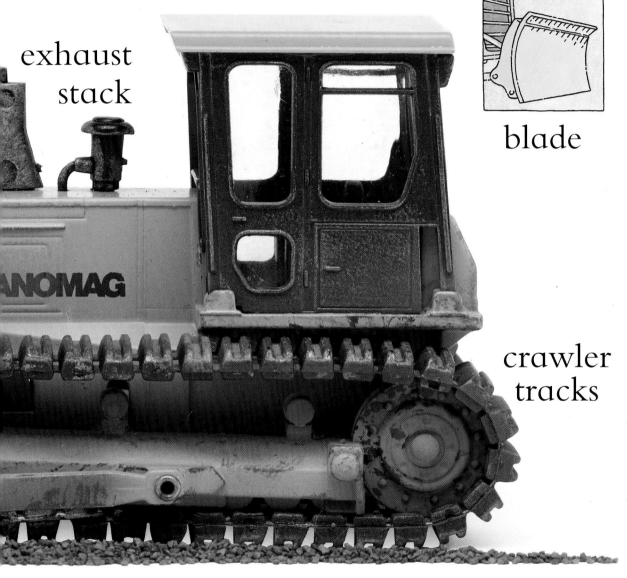

blade

crawler
tracks

ANOMAG

7

Excavator

arm

984

An excavator digs big holes.
The teeth on the bucket break
up the ground. Then the
bucket scoops up a load
and dumps it out
wherever it goes.

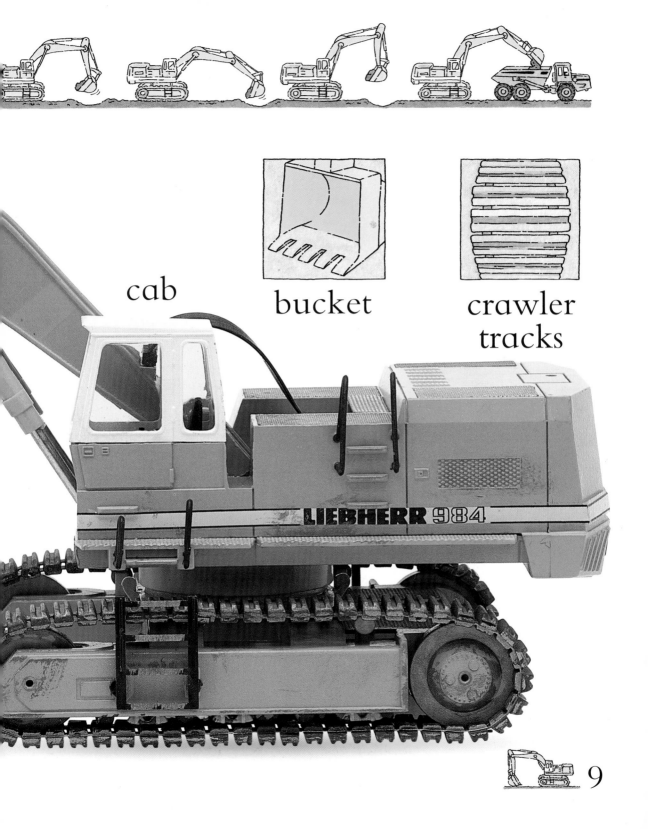

cab

bucket

crawler
tracks

LIEBHERR 984

9

Tilting dumper

This tilting dumper
can carry loads across
bumpy building sites.
The dumper body tilts
from side to side, so the
load stays steady. When it's
time to unload, the body
lifts up.

wheel

exhaust
stack

steering
wheel

steps

dumper body

Backhoe

This backhoe can do two jobs. It has a bucket at the back and a shovel at the front. The bucket digs small holes, such as trenches for pipes. The shovel pushes dirt back over the pipes. The legs keep the backhoe steady.

shovel

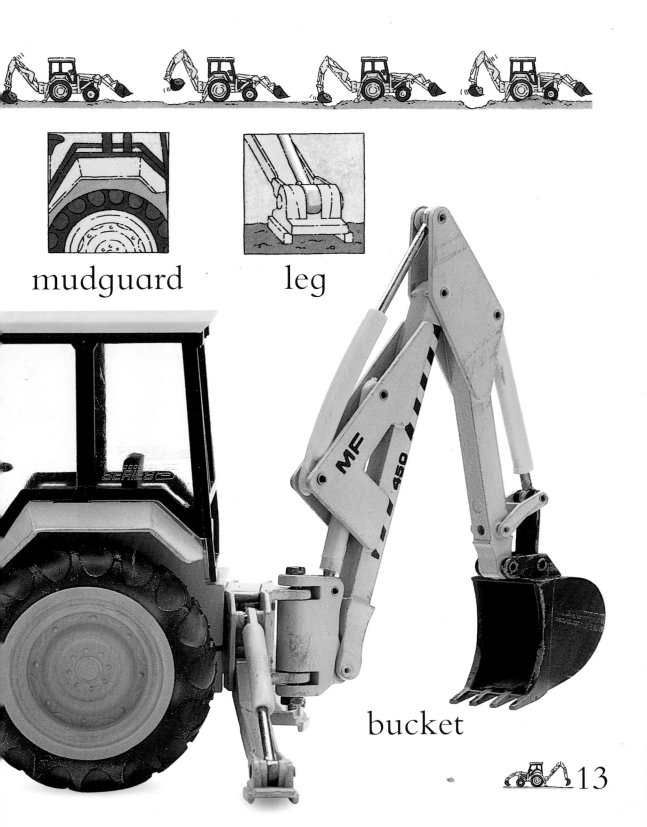

mudguard   leg

bucket

13

Dump truck

This dump truck brings loose materials like gravel or sand to a building site. When it's time to unload, powerful rams push the dumper body up. Then the tailboard swings open and the load tumbles out.

dumper
body

ATLAS

ram

tailboard

15

Forklift

A forklift carries heavy bricks, wood, or pipes around the building site. It has a moving arm with long forks on the end. The driver uses levers in the cab to slide the forks under the load and lift it up off the ground.

forks

arm

cab

levers

17

Tunneling loader

This loader scoops dirt up off the tunnel floor. The driver sits sideways. He can look forward as he drives into the tunnel, or backward when he drives out to dump the load. Powerful headlights light his way.

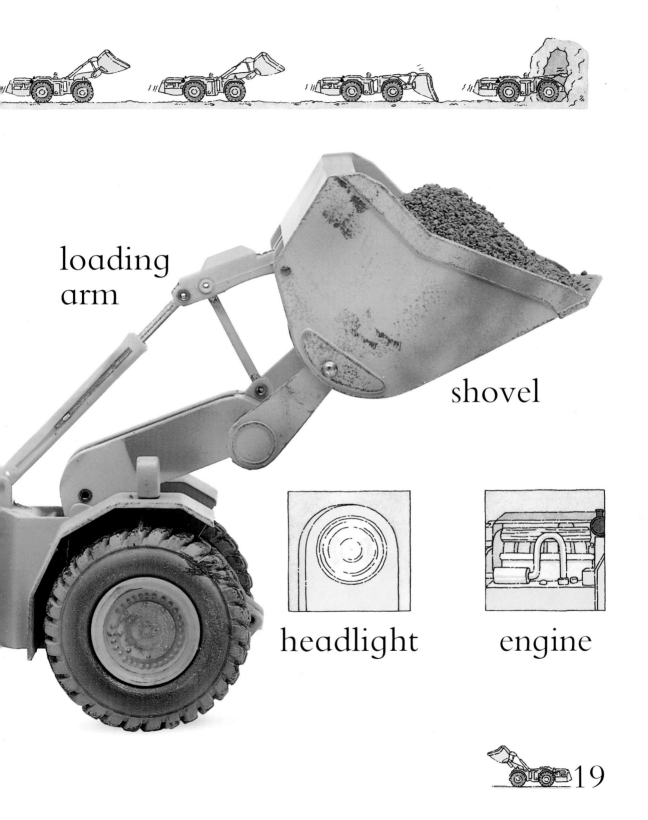

loading
arm

shovel

headlight

engine

19

Giant dump truck

This dump truck is so big that the driver has to climb a ladder to reach the cab. Giant dump trucks can carry heavy rocks and huge amounts of dirt. They are often used for building roads and tunnels.

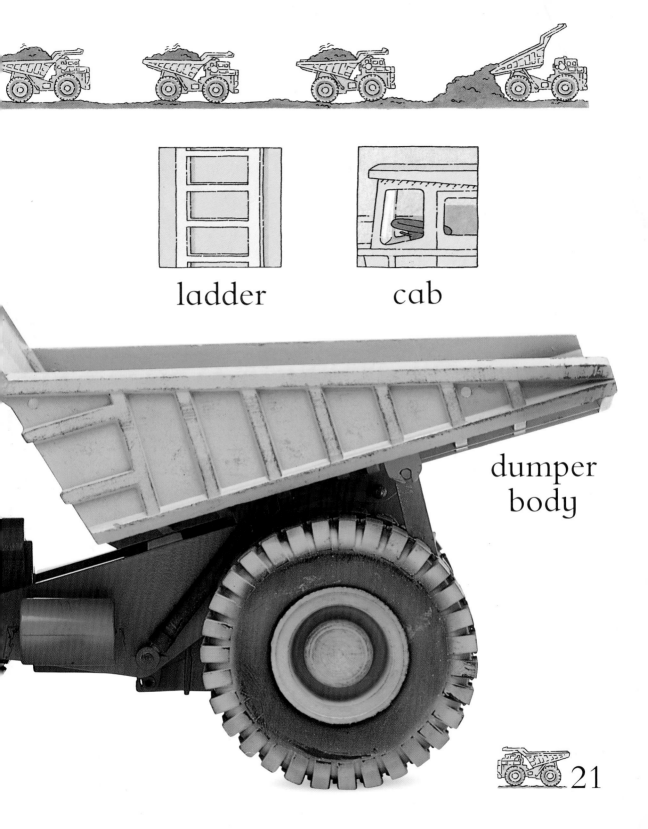

ladder

cab

dumper
body

21